THE ADVEN

PRISONERS
OF THE SUN

Little, Brown and Company
New York   Boston

Original Album: *Prisoners of the Sun*
Renewed Art Copyright © 1949, 1977 by Casterman, Belgium
Text Copyright © 1962 by Egmont UK Limited

Translated by Leslie Lonsdale-Cooper and Michael Turner

Additional Material
Art Copyright © Hergé/Moulinsart 2014
Text Copyright © Moulinsart 2014

casterman.com
tintin.com

Little, Brown and Company

Hachette Book Group
237 Park Avenue, New York, NY 10017
Visit our website at lb-kids.com

The publisher is not responsible for websites (or their content) that are not owned by the publisher.

First Edition: September 2014

ISBN: 978-0-316-40917-9

10 9 8 7 6 5 4 3 2 1

Printed in China

Tintin and Snowy

Brave reporter Tintin and his dog, Snowy, travel the world on exciting adventures.
No matter how dangerous things get, they always look out for each other.

Captain Haddock

Tintin's gruff friend, Captain Haddock, doesn't seem to get on very well with mother nature. In addition to his numerous run-ins with wild animals, the captain also manages to trigger an avalanche!

Thomson and Thompson

Throughout most of this story, police detectives Thomson and Thompson
are absolutely determined to find their friends.
But how successful they are is another matter.

Huascar

The Inca Huascar first shows up out of nowhere with a puzzling gift for Tintin.
Only later on does it become clear that the gesture had a very special meaning.

Zorrino

A young Peruvian orange seller, Zorrino is so grateful for Tintin saving him from bullies that he chooses to risk his life leading his new friend to the hidden kingdom of the Incas.

The Prince of the Sun

The Noble Prince of the Sun is the leader of a hidden Incan city.
He applies the ancient Incan laws fairly but firmly!

Professor Calculus

Tintin and his friends spend the whole adventure searching for Professor Calculus.
When at last they manage to find him, the professor doesn't seem
to realize the danger he's in!

PRISONERS OF THE SUN

At Police Headquarters in Callao, Peru . . .

Haddock, a retired ship's captain, and Tintin, the reporter? Oh, yes, Interpol warned me they'd be coming. Send them in.

As I understand it, this is the situation: your friend Professor Calculus has been kidnapped, and you have good reason to believe he's aboard the cargo ship "Pachacamac" – due to arrive in Callao any day now. Am I right?*

Absolutely.

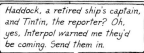

Well, gentlemen, as soon as the "Pachacamac" comes into port we will search the ship. If your friend really is aboard, then he will be restored to you immediately. Now, we can only . . .

Look down there; an Indian running away! . . . Someone was spying on us!

Surely you're mistaken . . .

No, no, I saw him quite clearly; an Indian, peering through the railings. He disappeared behind those bushes.

Bah! What does it matter? There was nothing confidential in   what we said.

Why not forget the whole incident . . . and allow me to offer you a glass of pisco? It's our national drink. Come, here's to the safe return of your friend Calculus.

* See The Seven Crystal Balls

A few minutes later . . .

Our lucky day! Just think, we're going to see old Cuthbert again! . . . This is the happiest day of my life! . . . Hurrah for pisco! It's all right! . . . Everything's going to be all right!

Perk up, don't look so gloomy. We'll soon see Cuthbert again. Things are looking up!

Yes, things are looking up . . . But you know, it doesn't alter the fact that we're being watched.

Pooh, that doesn't matter! Enjoy yourself. Look around you: the Indians, the clothes, the colours, the llamas.

Kilikilikili! . . . There's a nice little llama . . .

Hoity toity! Aren't we grand!

You be careful, señor . . .

Be careful? . . . Why? . . . I'm not going to eat your precious llama, am I? . . .

You're a nice little llama, aren't you? . . . You don't mind old Captain Haddock, do you?

When llama is angry, señor, he always do that.

And what manners!

Ungrateful brute! Animals like that shouldn't be allowed!

Perk up, Captain, don't look so gloomy. Remember, you said it yourself just now: things are looking up, we're going to see old Cuthbert again.

Hotel Cristobal Colon. Bueno . . .

The next morning . . .

RRRING

Hello . . . yes, Tintin speaking . . . Good morning, señor Chief Inspector . . . What? . . . The "Pachacamac" is in sight? . . . Fine! . . . Quay No. 24 . . . We'll be there right away.

A few minutes later . . .

There's the Chief Inspector with his men, down on the quayside . . .

But . . . I must be seeing things . . . Look!

Thomson and Thompson! What are those nitwits doing here?

You asked about your friends . . . well, here they come.

What a coincidence!

Not at all. These gentlemen were sent out by the C.I.D. to help in the search for your friend.

Now for the "Pachacamac". Where is she?

Out there, to the left of that little tug with the red funnel . . .

Ah, now I've got it . . . There she is . . . it's her all right . . . "Pachacamac" . . . let's hope old Calculus is on board!

Thundering typhoons!

?

Blistering barnacles! The "Pachacamac" is running up the yellow flag and a yellow and blue pennant: infectious disease on board!

Goodness gracious! And we've got to go on board to search the ship.

It's out of the question till the port health authorities have cleared her . . .

There goes the doctor's launch now, heading for the "Pachacamac" . . .

Well . . . we can only wait until they've finished.

I say, Captain, just what is that stuff, guano?

Guano? . . . Er . . . How shall I put it? . . .

PLOP

Guano? . . . Well, there's a free sample!

So you think that's funny, eh? . . . A brand new hat! . . . Ha ha; very amusing.

PLOP

Captain . . . The "Pachacamac" is hoisting more flags!

Billions of blue bubonic barnacles! She'll be quarantined!

Are they celebrating the Captain's birthday?

Putting a ship in quarantine, you landlubber, means keeping her in isolation for some time, to avoid risk of infection.

There's the launch coming back . . .

Well, doctor?

Two cases of yellow fever on board. I've ordered three weeks' quarantine.

You heard? . . . I'm terribly sorry about that . . . You'll just have to be patient.

Yes . . . obviously. Tell me, isn't that doctor an Indian?

A Quichua, as a matter of fact. Why?

Oh, no reason. I just wondered.

A little later . . .

Thundering typhoons! Three weeks . . . Three weeks without knowing whether Calculus is even aboard that blistering bathtub!

There's no question of waiting three weeks . . . We're going to find out tonight!

What do you mean, tonight?

Tonight I shall go aboard the "Pachacamac".

Tonight? . . . You? . . . What about the yellow fever, stupid? . . . Have you forgotten?

Captain, I'll bet anything you like that every man aboard the "Pachacamac" is as fit as you and me.

But thundering typhoons, the doctor definitely said . . .

The doctor is an Indian, Captain . . . a Quichua Indian . . . Doesn't that mean anything to you? . . .

Night has fallen . . .

Stop! We won't go any further . . .
We might be seen.

Right . . . You're quite sure?
I told you, there are sharks
around here . . .

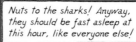

Nuts to the sharks! Anyway,
they should be fast asleep at
this hour, like everyone else!

Just as you
like . . .

There . . . You know the drill, don't you:
if I'm not back in a couple of hours,
inform the police . . . Goodbye, Captain.
And you be a good boy, Snowy.

Good luck,
Tintin.

Thundering typhoons! . . .
There's no stopping him!

Now comes the most
difficult part . . .

¿Qué pasa,
ahí abajo? . . .

¿Quien es?

Crumbs! Somebody else!

There's nothing for it . . . into this cabin, quick!

All's well, he didn't see me . . . He's going past . . .

¿Qué ha pasado, Chiquito? . . .

No es nada, debe de ser el gato . . .

Fine! They think it's a cat!

He's going back into his cabin . . . He's shut the door . . . Whew! . . .

ZZZZZ
ZZZZZ

Someone's in that bunk. I must get out of here!

Excuse me . . . A little further to the west!

There's only one person in the world who talks like that . . . and that is . . .

Cuthbert Calculus!

Professor! . . . Professor! . . . Wake up! . . . It's me, Tintin! Please, please wake up!

Nothing I can do . . . He's obviously been drugged!

Hello, whatever's that? . . . What's he got there, round his wrist?

The bracelet from the mummy!

Si, the bracelet of Rascar Capac!

Why, it's . . . it's Chiquito!

Si, Chiquito.

What do you want with poor Calculus?

He has committed sacrilege: he has put on the Inca bracelet! He must die! . . . As for you, you are a prisoner. I will decide later what your fate will be.

Alonzo!

You there! Stop!

Great snakes, another!

Quick, over the side!

Little devil, you will pay for this!

Thundering typhoons! . . . Those guano-gatherers are murdering Tintin!

Iconoclasts! . . . Pirates! . . . Just a few more strokes . . .

. . . and someone's going to get it in the neck!

?

Wooah! Wooah!

Blistering barnacles!

Wooah! Wooah!

And you shut up, you sealion, you!

Ah, there's Tintin.

Wooah!

Quick, climb aboard . . . Not hurt, are you?

No, not a scratch . . . But let's get out of here, fast!

Calculus is on board, Captain, I saw him. They're going to put him to death. They say he committed sacrilege by wearing an Inca bracelet.

Back to the shore! We must get reinforcements!

You dash back to the town and alert the police. I'll stay here and keep watch.

No sleep for us tonight, Snowy.

I might've guessed!

All quiet. But after what's happened they're bound to make a move . . . Yes, they're launching a boat. I hope the Captain gets help quickly . . .

A 'phone box, at last!

Hello . . . Yes . . . Police Headquarters . . . What? . . . You want to talk to the señor Chief Inspector? . . . At this hour? Have you gone crazy? . . . The señor Chief Inspector is asleep!

Thundering typhoons, I know that! If he wasn't asleep you wouldn't have to wake him up! . . . Tell him it's very, very urgent!

You're breaking my heart! . . . Look, it may be urgent, but nobody wakes the señor Chief Inspector at four a.m.!

But you must wake him, I tell you, it's . . . Hello . . . Hello . . . Hello . . . The blistering blundering bird-brain, he's hung up!

Meanwhile . . .

The boat's getting nearer . . . Come on, Snowy, but don't show yourself. We're going to take a closer look at them . . .

I've got an idea . . . I'll ring up the Thompsons . . . Four, two, eight . . . That's it . . .

That sounds like the telephone.

To be precise: the telephone.

Great snakes . . . They're carrying Calculus ashore!

RRRRING

Are you going to answer it?

Me? . . . Certainly not . . . how can I? I'm asleep!

Taking their time, the baboons!

RRRRING

You can't be asleep, you're talking to me!

You know very well that I talk in my sleep!

Blue blistering barnacles! I can't stand here all night!

Very well, I'll go. But next time, it's your turn!

Hello? . . . Hello, Thomson? . . . And about time too! . . . This is Captain Haddock . . .

What? . . . Who? . . . Oh, yes, Captain Haddock . . . I . . . What? . . . Calculus? . . . Where? . . . Yes . . . Right . . . We'll come at once . . .

Half an hour later . . .

Nearly two hours since I left him . . . I hope he's all right.

There's our boat . . . I left Tintin here . . . But where is he?

Hi, Tintin!

Tintin!

Tintin!

No use shouting ourselves hoarse. Tintin's gone. We must examine the beach; we ought to pick up his tracks quite quickly.

It's like looking for a needle in a haystack.

To be precise: we look like needles in a haystack.

Here, look at this! Footprints!

And others here. Look, there were several men, with horses . . . no, llamas . . . See these marks in the sand . . .

Come on. This way . . . it's plain sailing . . .

The footprints stop at the road . . . Still, no matter, it's obvious they kept going in the same direction.

Just a minute . . . What if it's a trick . . . Supposing they went in the opposite direction?

Quite right! . . . I submit that half of us should go one way, and half the other.

What a brilliant idea! There are three of us: half of three is one and a half . . .

Great Scotland Yard! You're right! What can we do?

You two go your way, and I'll go mine . . . And we'll see which of us finds Tintin . . . Goodbye . . . And keep your eyes open!

Don't worry, they're wide open!

To be precise: they're . . .

BLIND CORNER!

Many hours later . . .

Here, boy . . . Have you met anyone along this road – a young European, with a white dog?

?

Yes . . . and I've met him before!

Tintin! . . . You young rascal, you had me properly fooled! . . . Honestly, I'd never have recognised you . . . But why the disguise?

Come along . . . I'll explain.

Shortly after you left they brought Calculus ashore. They had accomplices waiting on the beach. They lifted Calculus on to a llama and led him away. I followed at a distance, making sure they didn't spot me . . .

We came to Santa Clara, a small town. I hastily bought this cap and poncho in the market, so I was able to get close to them at the station and see them buy tickets to Jauga . . .

What did they do with Calculus?

Obviously they'd drugged him; he followed them like a sleep-walker . . . Then the train left – without me, alas: I hadn't enough money for a ticket. After that I retraced my steps, hoping to find you . . .

Thundering typhoons! . . . The gangsters! Going off with Calculus! . . . But we'll catch the next train . . .

Of course! But unfortunately the train only runs every other day.

But why are you by yourself? Where are the police? Didn't you telephone them?

Still in bed . . . And the Thompsons are hot on your trail, somewhere . . .

Two days later . . .

Our seats are in the last coach, aren't they?

Si, señor.

Lucky we arrived in good time: the train's going to be crammed.

No, no - it is impossible . . . You ask too much . . . I cannot . . .

It is his order - and you know what happens to those who disobey him . . .

Half an hour later . . .

TOOOT

We're off . . . How odd: all that crowd of passengers, but not a soul has got into our compartment.

RESERVED

Have a good trip, señores!

The train steams on for several hours . . .

Excuse me: I'll be back in a minute.

It's a funny thing . . . D'you know, we're absolutely alone in this carriage.

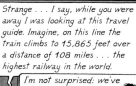

Strange . . . I say, while you were away I was looking at this travel guide. Imagine, on this line the train climbs to 15,865 feet over a distance of 108 miles . . . the highest railway in the world.

I'm not surprised: we've been going up steadily.

Hello, we're slowing down . . . I expect we're coming to a station.

Captain, get out, quick! The coupling has broken and our coach is running away!

Quick, jump!

My turn . . . Now for it!

Great snakes! I've forgotten . . .

Billions of blistering barnacles! Why doesn't he jump?

Crumbs! A tunnel! Snowy! Snowy!

Oww!

Snowy! . . . Snowy!

Tintin! . . . Where is Tintin?

?

CRASH CRACK

Oh, look! . . . The coach has gone over the edge . . . We just made it!

!

We can thank our lucky stars we got out of that, Snowy!

You're telling me!

First let's get dry . . . Then we must try to find the Captain . . .

Come on Snowy, one last effort, you're nearly there.

Now, on our way. We must join up with the Captain.

Still no sign . . . Was he hurt when he jumped?

What has become of him?

Hooray!

Hooray!

Safe and sound! What an escape!

TOOOOT

Hey, stop! . . . Arrêtez! . . . Whoa!

You were in the runaway coach? . . . You were able to jump in time? . . . How fortunate!

I am in charge at the next station . . . When the train arrived we found a coach missing . . . I was most upset: it is the first accident we have had on this line . . .

Accident? . . . You mean attempted murder!

Attempted murder? . . . But that is impossible!

All the same, it's true. But don't let's waste time. We were going to Jauga . . . Will you take us there?

Some hours later, in Jauga . . .

A short man, you say, with a little black beard, and glasses? . . . Yes, I think . . . Wait . . . He was accompanied by some Indians, wasn't he?

You mean he was a prisoner of the Indians. Our friend has been kidnapped.

Kidnapped by the Indians? . . . I . . . er . . . No, he wasn't the man you're looking for . . . The one I'm talking about seemed to be following the Indians quite willingly.

Naturally; he'd been drugged.

You think so? . . . That is not very likely . . . But now I come to think of it, the man . . . Yes, the man I saw was tall, and fair . . . and clean-shaven.

But you told us yourself, just a moment ago . . .

I was mistaken, that's all . . . I am sorry I can be of no further assistance to you, gentlemen . . . The interview is closed!

! !

Why that sudden change? . . . Curious . . . He seemed anxious not to be involved. Is he afraid of the Indians?

Only one thing to do: split up and question some of the locals.

Right! . . . We'll meet outside the station in an hour.

A short man, with a little beard, and wearing glasses . . . you see him?

No sé!

Short man . . . little beard . . . glasses . . . You see him?

No sé!

You see him?

No sé!

No sé! No sé! . . . They're the only words they know, the stubborn South American centipedes!

?

Por favor, kind señor.

No sé!

?

Meanwhile . . .

No sé! No sé! . . . That's a fat lot of good! They must know something . . . But they seem to be afraid . . .

Oh well, I'll ask that young orange-seller . . .

No sé I'll bet!

Here comes Zorrino . . . Hold everything: this'll be rich!

Ha! ha! ha! ha!

Ha! ha! ha! ha!

Ha! ha! ha! ha!

Ha! ha! ha! ha!

Lost something, sonny boy?

Aaaaah!

Brute!

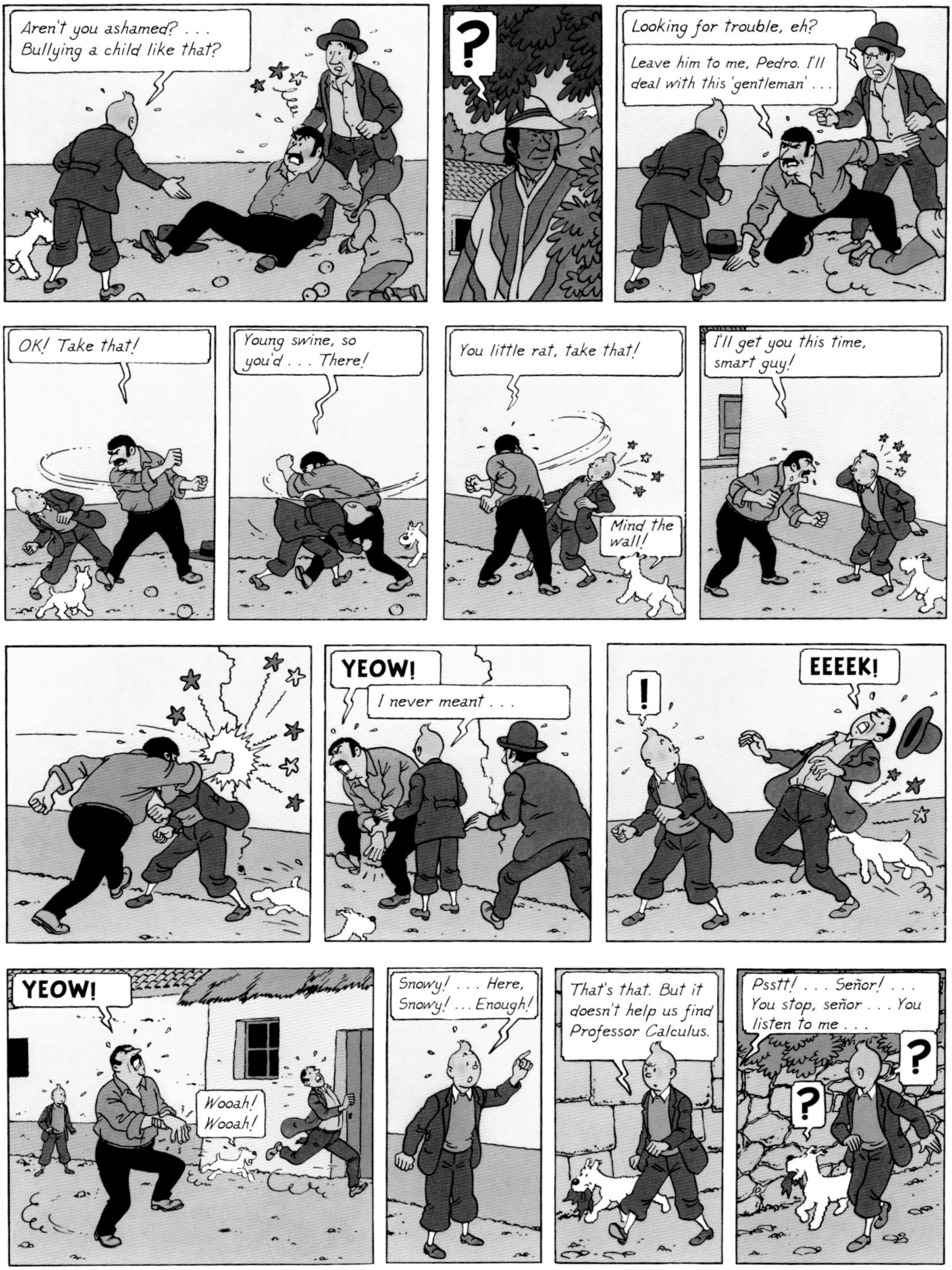
Aren't you ashamed? . . . Bullying a child like that?
?
Looking for trouble, eh?
Leave him to me, Pedro. I'll deal with this 'gentleman' . . .
OK! Take that!
Young swine, so you'd . . . There!
You little rat, take that!
Mind the wall!
I'll get you this time, smart guy!
YEOW!
I never meant . . .
!
EEEEK!
YEOW!
Wooah! Wooah!
Snowy! . . . Here, Snowy! . . . Enough!
That's that. But it doesn't help us find Professor Calculus.
Psstt! . . . Señor! . . . You stop, señor . . . You listen to me . . .
?
?

You not look this way . . . You tie up your shoelace . . .

I know where your friend is prisoner . . . You buy guns and come tomorrow, at sunrise, to Bridge of the Inca . . . You understand? . . . Bridge of the Inca . . . You go now.

Fantastic! A guide straight out of the blue!

What if it's a trap?

You listen to me, señor . . .

?

?

I see you go to help Indian boy . . . You are good . . . You are brave . . .

Er . . . I . . . Who are you?

I speak wise words . . . You not go in search of your friend, otherwise you meet many dangers.

How do you know?

I know, señor . . . You remember train that ran away . . . You have good luck that time . . . But you not always have good luck . . . You listen to me: you not go . . .

I can't abandon my friend - but thank you, anyway.

That is very foolish choice . . . You still go, then take this . . . Very good, help you in danger . . .

A little medal . . . a talisman. What do you . . .

!

Next morning, at dawn . . .

Blistering barnacles, why doesn't he show up, this guide of yours?

Pssst . . . Psssst!

!

!

Quick, señores! . . . You come now!

Careful, be on your guard!

20

Why, it's the little orange-seller . . . the one I told you about.

So it was you . . .

Yes, I talk to you yesterday, from behind wall . . . If Indians see me speak to you, they kill me at once . . . You come now . . .

You wait for me on other side of bridge . . . I come back quick.

Where's he off to?

I don't know. He told us to wait.

Thundering typhoons! Llamas!

To carry supplies, señores . . . Journey very long!

This is too much! . . . If you think I'm travelling around with this pair of perambulating fire-pumps, you're very much mistaken!

Llamas very gentle, señor. You not be afraid.

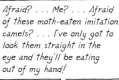

Afraid? . . . Me? . . . Afraid of these moth-eaten imitation camels? . . . I've only got to look them straight in the eye and they'll be eating out of my hand!

Like that . . . there!

YEEEEOW!

You miserable iconoclast!

You not hit him, señor.

21

When llama angry . . .

Blistering barnacles, I know! . . . When llama angry, he always do that!

Come on, we've wasted enough time . . . Are we ready, er . . .? Look, we don't even know your name . . .

Zorrino, señor.

Now look, Zorrino: where is our friend? . . . And why would none of the Indians tell us, though they all seemed to know what had happened to him?

He is prisoner in Temple of the Sun . . . But no one tell . . . all afraid.

Afraid? Of whom?

Afraid of Inca, señor. Vengeance of Inca terrible when Indian tell white man what white man must not know.

The Inca? . . . The Temple of the Sun? . . . An Inca, in these days? . . . It's unbelievable.

White men not know, señor. Only you know.

Thanks to you, Zorrino; but aren't you afraid of the Inca, too?

Alone, I afraid: with you, I not afraid!

That evening . . .

There is chulpa, señor, old Inca tomb. We spend night there, go on again in morning.

I'll stand the first watch. At about midnight I'll wake you, and you can take over.

Right.

Good night, Captain. And don't forget to wake me in good time.

Don't worry, I will . . . Sleep well, both of you.

Good night, Zorrino.

Good night, señor Tintin.

Amazing! An Inca plant in bloom!

Excuse me, señor Inca, but have you a licence for that gun?

A licence? . . . Sacrilege! Sacrilege! . . . The fire of heaven will strike you down!

Ugh! What a horrible nightmare! . . . It's just a ray of sunlight . . . But . . .

Good heavens, they let me sleep on . . . Captain! . . . I say, Captain! Ahoy there! . . .

Captain! . . . Captain! . . . Zorrino! . . .

. . . orrino!

. . . orrino!

Nothing . . . only the echo . . . What's become of them?

Having breakfast, I'll bet!

I don't like it: I'd better get my gun!

Great snakes! My gun: it's vanished!

Zorrino's cap; otherwise, not a trace of them . . .

WOOAH! WOOAH! WOOAH!

Quick! What has Snowy found?

WOOAH! WOOAH!

Captain! What in the world . . .

Cut the cackle and get me out of this before I go crazy!

?

Billions of blistering . . . I . . . I . . .

Hooray! Got it!

This miserable reptile has spent the night waltzing along my spine!

A lizard!

Careful!

Hey, look! It's dropping to bits!

WOOAH! WOOAH!

WOOAH! WOOAH!

Now, Captain, what happened?

Well, it was getting on towards midnight and I was walking up and down to keep warm. Suddenly a shadow rose up in front of me. There wasn't time to move a muscle before . . . Wham! . . . I felt a violent blow on the head . . . Next thing I knew, I was where you found me: tied up and gagged, with that lizard down my neck. What about Zorrino?

He's vanished, Captain, and so have the llamas, and our supplies. Much more serious, our guns have gone too!

Our guns? . . . The gangsters! . . . Bandits! . . . Filibusters! . . . Pirates! . . .

Thundering typhoons, what do we do now?

First of all, we must try to find Zorrino . . . Then tackle whoever's kidnapped him.

Snowy! . . .
Here, Snowy!

It's up to you now, Snowy . . .
We've got to find Zorrino.
Look, here's his cap . . .
Go on! . . . Seek him!

Come on! . . . After him!

WOOAH!
WOOAH!

Hey, not so fast, you
mountain goat, you!

Two hours later . . .

Stop! There
they are!

The path doubles back down
there . . . They'll pass directly
below us . . .

If we took a short cut down
the cliff we could surprise
them . . . Stay here, Snowy
. . . Come on, Captain!

We'll break our
necks, that's
a certainty!

Find some other way,
Captain: this is too steep.

Just in time! . . . Here they come! . . .
Careful, not a sound now . . .

?

HELP!

! ?

Hooray!

Come past me, Captain, while I cover you. You lot stay put!

Now then, get going down that path . . . fast! The first one who stops or comes back is a dead duck! . . . OK? . . . On your way . . . and take your pal with you!

I said fast!

Is no hurry . . .

BANG

CRACK

I think they've got the idea! Now I'll rejoin the others.

You see, Zorrino, we didn't abandon you.

I know you save me. Where is Snowy?

We left him higher up: he couldn't climb down . . . Look, there he is.

Hello, Snowy!

Wooah! Wooah!

?

Wooah! Wooah!

I've got a real bird's eye view!

Ooh! A condor!

!

Wooaaah!

Thundering typhoons!

Heavens! What can we do? . . . I daren't shoot . . .

Snowy! Oh, poor, poor Snowy!

WOOAH!

There . . . look . . . it's settled on a rock . . . Now or never! . . . Blistering barnacles, Tintin, be careful!

BANG

Hooray!

Quickly now! Ropes, and my scarf . . . I must go after Snowy . . .

You can't go up there!

You don't think I'd leave Snowy, Captain? . . . Injured, dying even . . .

Tintin, it's suicide, I tell you!

Snowy! . . . Snowy! . . . No answer!

Snowy! . . . Snowy!

Not a sound!

Oh, it's you? . . . I say, these birds certainly know how to treat a guest!

!?

28

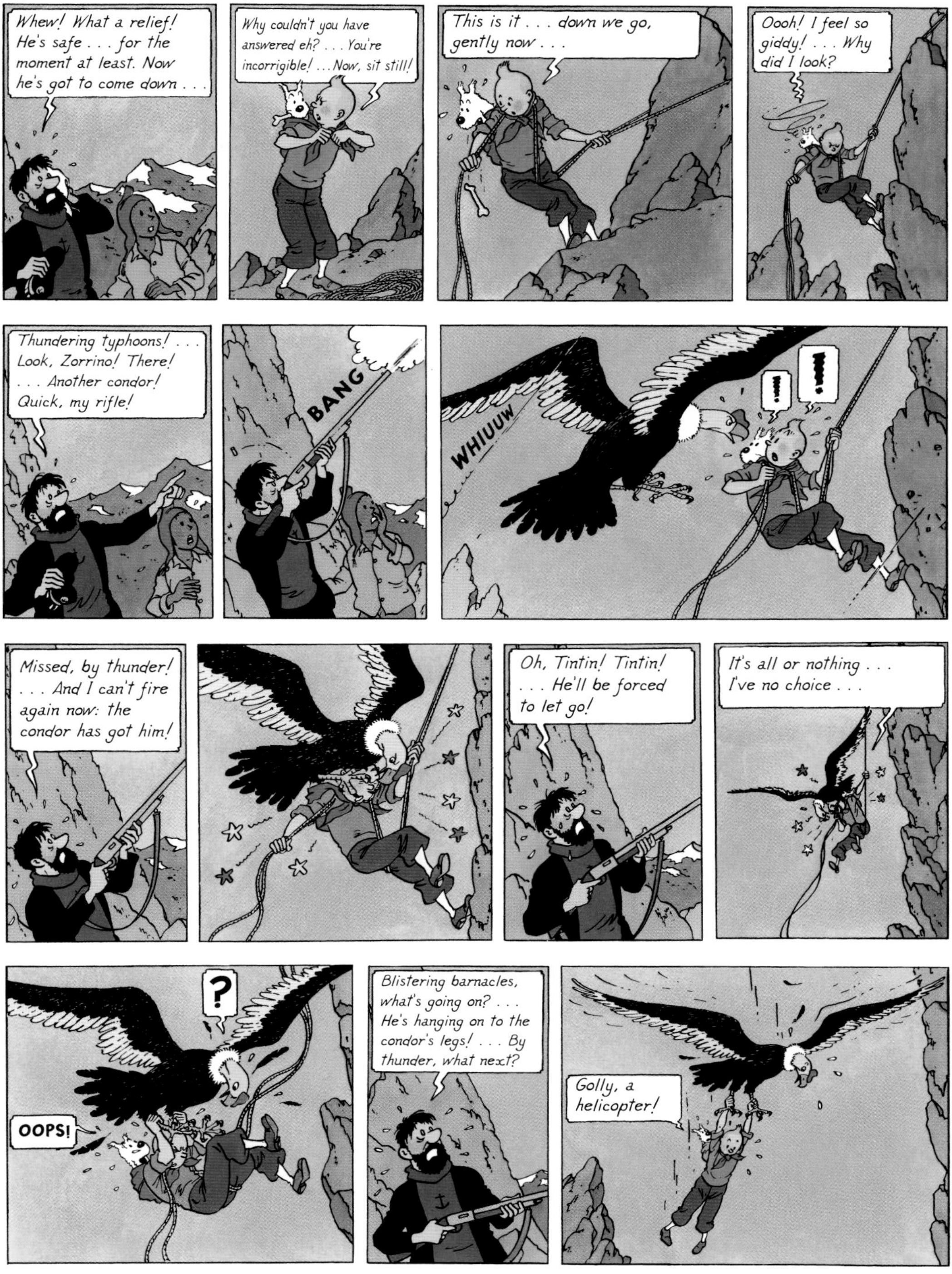

Whew! What a relief! He's safe . . . for the moment at least. Now he's got to come down . . .
Why couldn't you have answered eh? . . . You're incorrigible! . . . Now, sit still!
This is it . . . down we go, gently now . . .
Oooh! I feel so giddy! . . . Why did I look?
Thundering typhoons! . . . Look, Zorrino! There! . . . Another condor! Quick, my rifle!
BANG
WHIUUW
!
!!!
Missed, by thunder! . . . And I can't fire again now: the condor has got him!
Oh, Tintin! Tintin! . . . He'll be forced to let go!
It's all or nothing . . . I've no choice . . .
?
OOPS!
Blistering barnacles, what's going on? . . . He's hanging on to the condor's legs! . . . By thunder, what next?
Golly, a helicopter!

Saved!

Pirate! . . . Doryphore! . . . Gobbledygook! Just wait till I get you to the taxidermist, you bald-headed budgerigar!

A little later . . .

Blistering barnacles, what a country! . . . Is there no end to this mountainous menagerie?

Is it far now, Zorrino?

Far, señor, very far! . . . Still long journey to Temple of the Sun . . . Many days . . . Must cross high mountains, much snow . . .

Days go by . . .

One morning . . .

Narrow gully, señor . . . Is very dangerous . . . You not make noise, you not speak . . . otherwise avalanche come . . .

OK, little'un. We'll watch it.

Brrr! It's freezing! . . . You bet I'll catch a cold . . . There, what did I say? . . . Aaah! . . . Aaaaah! . . .

AAAAAAH . . .

TCHOOO

BRRROOM BRRROOM

An avalanche!

?

30

Quick! . . .
Behind this rock!

Whew! That's better
. . . It was a near
thing . . . Quick, I
must dig Zorrino out!

Where llamas? . . . And Captain?

I don't know, Zorrino . . .
Buried somewhere under
the snow . . . We must
find them.

Captain! . . .
Captain!

Careful! . . .
You not shout!

Crumbs! You're right! . . .
Will it . . .? No, nothing's
moving now.

!

Wooah!
Wooah!

The Captain! . . . He's found
the Captain!

Come on! To work! . . .
Where is he?

There!

No sign of life! . . .
We must get him out
. . . and quickly!

Poor Captain! Frozen stiff!

!

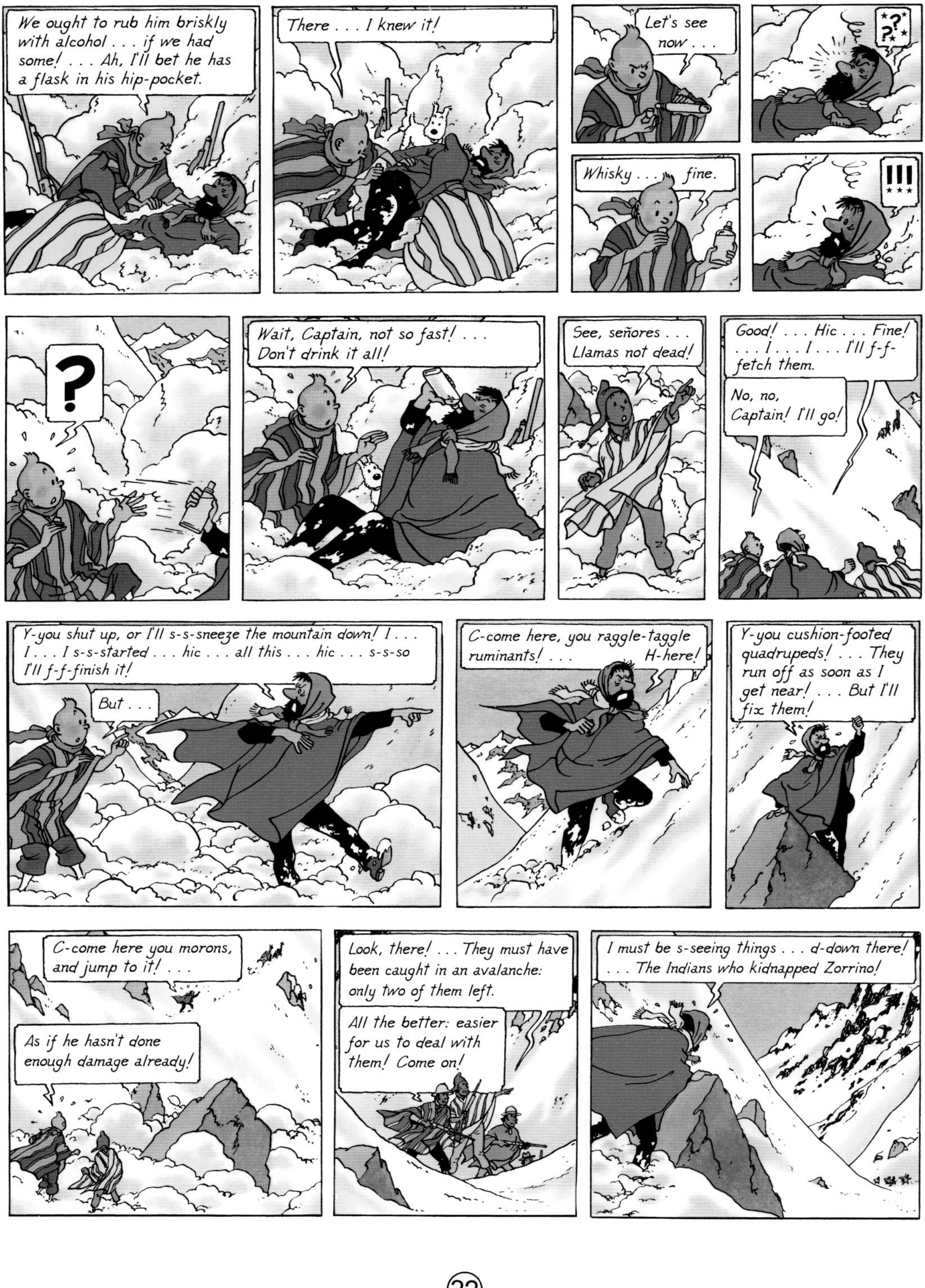

We ought to rub him briskly with alcohol . . . if we had some! . . . Ah, I'll bet he has a flask in his hip-pocket.
There . . . I knew it!
Let's see now . . .
Whisky . . . fine.
Wait, Captain, not so fast! . . . Don't drink it all!
See, señores . . . Llamas not dead!
Good! . . . Hic . . . Fine! . . . I . . . I . . . I'll f-f-fetch them.
No, no, Captain! I'll go!
Y-you shut up, or I'll s-s-sneeze the mountain down! I . . . I . . . I s-s-started . . . hic . . . all this . . . hic . . . s-s-so I'll f-f-finish it!
But . . .
C-come here, you raggle-taggle ruminants! . . . H-here!
Y-you cushion-footed quadrupeds! . . . They run off as soon as I get near! . . . But I'll fix them!
C-come here you morons, and jump to it! . . .
As if he hasn't done enough damage already!
Look, there! . . . They must have been caught in an avalanche: only two of them left.
All the better: easier for us to deal with them! Come on!
I must be s-seeing things . . . d-down there! . . . The Indians who kidnapped Zorrino!

Get going,
filibusters! . . .
Buzz off,
you weevils!

Be off with you,
slubberdegullions!

What's he shouting
at now? Let's see.

Patagonians! . . .
Bashi-bazouks! . . .
Carpet-sellers! . . .
Kleptomaniacs! . . .

Go on! . . .
Fire!

Wait till he
gets closer.

Great snakes! Those Indians
again! . . . Bolting like
rabbits! . . . But the
Captain . . . He's
done for!

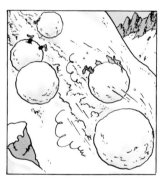

You know, Zorrino, the Captain's guardian angel has a full-time job!

Nothing broken, Captain? . . . That's lucky . . . Well, I reckon we've seen the last of those ruffians . . . Now, let's get back to the path . . .

Yes, yes . . .

I say, where's Snowy? . . . I don't remember seeing him around for quite a while . . . Snowy! . . . Snowy! . . .

Snowy! . . . Snowy!! . . . Where has he got to?

Good old Snowy! You've managed to dig out the Captain's cap.

We've found your cap; that's fine. But I'm afraid we've lost the llamas, and that means no more food, and no more ammunition . . .

No more ammunition?

You needn't worry about that. Look: two boxes of cartridges, here in my pocket.

What a bit of luck! If needs be we can shoot for the pot . . . And take care of that newspaper: we might need it to light a fire.

Many hours later . . .

You see, down there. Tomorrow we come into thick jungle.

Is the Temple of the Sun in the forest?

No, señor, temple still far away. We go through jungle. Then more mountains.

Blistering barnacles! Is there no end to it? I've had about enough of this little jaunt, I can tell you!

Stop! . . . Look, there's a cave! . . . Why don't we spend the night here?

Perhaps, but . . .

Don't worry. I'll look it over first.

It's OK!

It's all right . . . You can come on up . . . It's very snug.

What? . . . What is it? . . . What are you waving your arms for?

What? . . . Who? . . . What did you say? . . . Shout louder, I can't hear you!

What? . . . Thundering typhoons, speak up, can't you!

There's a bear behind you!

!!!

Next morning . . .

All well, Captain?

No it isn't! This thundering country - it's entirely populated by man-eating mosquitoes!

Blue blistering barnacles! Got you, bloodsucker!

HA-HA-HA-HA-HA-HA

HA-HA-HA-HA-HA-HA

!

CRACK CRACK CRACK

Tell me the truth. I can take it. I've been run over by a bus, haven't I?

Rubbish, Captain. It was a tapir.

When tapir in hurry, señor, tapir go straight on. He not worry for things in path. But tapir is not wicked, señor, not hard to tame him.

I'm glad to hear it. All the same, I'll use my gun to tame the next joker who comes along.

I can tell you one thing. Next time I need a nice, restful holiday. I'll know exactly where to come!

Ouch! These beastly mosquitoes!

Here is clearing. Good place to spend night.

Excellent idea . . .

Darkness falls . . .

Next day, at dawn . . .

ZZZZZ

ZZZZZ ZZZZZ ZZZZZ

!

Mmmm . . . Snowy . . . Go away, Snowy . . . Leave me alone . . .

?

EEK! HELP!

Hop it, you four-legged Cyrano!

Calm down, Captain: it's only a poor old ant-eater who wanted to say good-morning.

You covered with ants . . . Him look for breakfast.

The days go by . . .

Very soon, big river . . . We must cross . . .

How? Do we swim?

Bloodsuckers!

You wait here, señor . . . Zorrino come back soon . . .

Right.

How odd. Look at all those tree-trunks floating down the river.

Tree-trunks? Don't you believe it! They're alligators!

Alligators! . . . Good heavens! I could have sworn . . .

A natural mistake . . . They don't fool me.

TINTIN! HELP!

I . . . er . . . thanks, Tintin . . . er . . . you see, I . . .

Quite, Captain! Anyway, he's quite harmless now . . . just like a tree-trunk.

CRACK

It's all right . . . It was only Zorrino breaking a dead branch.

You come, señores. I find canoe.

See . . .

Watch out, shipmates, this is going to be hot! . . . Here they come! They've spotted us!

BANG

BANG

BANG

!

BANG

BANG

Loathsome brutes! Let me polish them off!

No, no! It's a waste of ammunition.

This beastly steaming jungle! . . . Will it never end?

Tomorrow we leave forest, señor Captain.

The following evening . . .

We camp here tonight . . . Up there, in mountains, is Temple of the Sun.

Off we go! . . . I say, where did you find that rope?

For certain we need ropes . . . I make them from jungle creepers.

What a torrent! We can't cross here: we'll have to try further up. The Temple of the Sun certainly has good defences!

Two days later . . .

There's nothing for it, Captain: this is the only place . . . You see that spike of rock over there . . . We must try to lasso it with a rope.

Right!

Here goes!

Hooray! Got it!

OK. I've fastened this end to a tree . . . Now, who's first?

Zorrino, with señor Tintin's gun, to test rope!

He's got guts, that boy!

Be careful, Zorrino!

Is OK!

Fine . . . my turn next . . .

Thundering typhoons! You need a cool head for this!

Blue blistering barnacles!

40

For heaven's sake, Captain, you'll fall . . . Leave your cap!

And buy another at the local hatter's, I suppose?

Whew! Done it!

Now it's my turn.

Oooh! Let's stop playing Tarzan!

Don't be silly, Snowy . . . We'll be all right . . .

Wooooah!

Help!

41

Tintin!
Tintin!

He's gone . . . I can't see him . . . But . . . it's impossible . . . He's an excellent swimmer . . . he'll come to the surface.

Not a sign . . . It's all over . . . He's drowned . . . It's too dreadful, I can't believe it . . .

!

Drowned? . . . Drowned? . . . Señor Tintin not dead, is he, Captain?

Alas, Zorrino!

My poor Zorrino. Tintin has gone. We shall never see him again.

Cooee!

?

?

That voice . . . It can't be . . . I must be dreaming . . .

No, no! Is señor Tintin?

Captain! Zorrino!

Tintin! . . . Tintin! . . . Is it really you? . . . Where are you?

Wooah! Wooah!

Here, behind the waterfall.

Behind the waterfall? . . . How can you be behind the waterfall?

Come down. You'll see! . . .

?

Climb down . . . Lower . . .

Come closer! . . . Now, watch the foot of the waterfall. I'm going to throw a stone to show where I am.

There!

! !

You saw it? . . . Good! . . . Now, go up and get the rope. Tie a big stone on the end, and throw it to me . . . I think I've made a very interesting discovery!

Right!

That's tight enough . . . I'll sling it to you.

Splendid!

Secure the end of the rope to a rock. I'll do the same at this end.

OK.

All fast here!

Fine! Now, come on and join me here.

?

W-w-what? . . . We join you? . . . Don't you mean the other way round?

No, no! Hang on tight to the rope and plunge through the waterfall . . . You'll see, it's only a thin curtain of water.

But . . . but . . . you're quite sure . . .

Yes, yes! Come on!

Davy Jones, here I come!

You see?

!

Blistering barnacles! Where are we?

Wait while I call Zorrino . . .

It's incredible! . . . Extraordinary! . . . Amazing! . . . Fantastic!

Your turn, Zorrino!

There you are!

!

All together again, Zorrino!

Tintin! . . . Oh, Tintin! . . . Zorrino was so afraid. . . You not hurt?

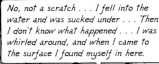

No, not a scratch . . . I fell into the water and was sucked under . . . Then I don't know what happened . . . I was whirled around, and when I came to the surface I found myself in here.

It seems incredible, but I think I've stumbled on an entrance to the Temple of the Sun . . . so ancient that even the Incas themselves have probably forgotten all about it . . . Anyway, we'll soon see.

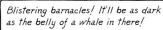

Blistering barnacles! It'll be as dark as the belly of a whale in there!

I thought so too, But I had a look. The rock is covered with some sort of phosphorescence which gives a little light. Shall we go?

No noise, now! . . . Careful! . . . I've got a hunch we're nearly at the end of our journey.

Calculus, here we come!

Where's this leading us?

If we keep going we'll soon see . . .

Now we're in trouble . . . The passage is blocked . . . There's no way of getting through.

The roof-fall was probably caused by an earthquake: they're pretty frequent in South America . . . Anyway, we're sunk now . . . unless . . .

Wooah! Wooah!

I've found the emergency exit!

Snowy seems to be on to something . . . It looks as though there's a way through there. Hold these, Zorrino, I'm going to try . . .

Any good?

I hope so.

OK?

So far so good . . .

?

I've just emerged in a sort of grotto . . . I'll see if there's any way of . . . OH!

Heavens! What's up?

!

I . . . um . . . er . . . Nice day, isn't it?

You . . . er . . . you speak English? . . . No? . . . ¿Habla usted español? No? . . . Well, er . . . parlez-vous français? . . . Oh dear . . .

Great snakes! What a fool I've been . . . of course you don't speak.

?

Crumbs! Look what's tumbled down . . . the contents of a tomb!

My guess about an earthquake was right . . . Let's see what's beyond . . .

?

Inca mummies! We certainly are in a tomb!

It might be possible to push this slab over . . . But I can't do it alone . . . I'll call the others . . .

This chap looks pretty poorly.

Hey, Captain! . . . Zorrino! . . . Here, I need your help.

Right, we're coming.

You go first, Zorrino. Then I'll pass you the guns and the ponchos.

You give me guns, señor Captain.

Here you are.

Here guns, Tintin.

Thanks, Zorrino.

Oh! Place of dead men, here!

Yes, Zorrino, there is no other way . . .

It's my turn now . . .

! ? TOOOOT

Crumbs! That noise came from Snowy! What happened?

Golly! Whatever next? A musical bone!

Dead man's flute, Tintin . . . Incas make pipes from bones and put in tomb.

A flute carved out of a tibia . . . And Snowy blew it by mistake . . .

Hey, Captain, where are you?

Blistering barnacles! A tomb! . . . This is cheerful, I must say!

There wasn't any other way through, Captain.

Look here, did you drag me along just to meet these two jolly zombies?

No, no, Captain. There's something else. I'm sure we're nearly there. You see this slab? We must try to push it over. Behind it there might be . . .

What a hope!

Come on now . . . One . . . two . . . three . . . Heave!

Splendid! . . . It moved! . . . Again: one . . . two . . . three . . . Heave!

!

Sacrilege! . . . Seize them!

Stand back, anachronisms! . . . Keep off, you imitation Incas, you!

Tramps! . . . Zapotecs! . . . Pockmarks! . . . Pithecanthropuses! . . . Bashi-bazouks! . . . Let me go, you savages!

Good! Now, hold them prisoner until we bring them before the Inca!

Sea-gherkins! . . . Ectoplasms! . . . Poltroons! . . . Politicians! . . . Doryphores! . . . Terrorists!

Don't cry, Zorrino . . . We'll get out of this, you'll see . . .

Get out? Easier said than done . . . Poor Zorrino!

Hello, what's this at the bottom of my pocket?

Ah, yes, the little coin that Indian gave me in Jauga . . . I'd forgotten all about it.

"You still go, then take this . . . Very good, help you in danger."

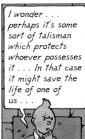

I wonder . . . perhaps it's some sort of talisman which protects whoever possesses it . . . In that case it might save the life of one of us . . .

Look, Zorrino, here's something for you . . . Take good care of it: it might be very useful.

You come . . . The Inca waits.

Oho! He waits, does he? . . . Well, I've got a thing or two to say to his lordship!

Keep calm, Captain! Keep calm, I implore you . . .

Great snakes! The Inca!

Look at that Indian on the left . . . It's Chiquito, General Alcazar's music-hall partner . . . The man I saw on the "Pachacamac".

Strangers, it is our command that you reveal by what trickery you have entered the Temple of the Sun.

I . . . er . . . Noble Prince of the Sun, we found the entrance quite by chance, when I was swept into a waterfall.

Be that as it may, our laws decree but one penalty. Those who violate the sacred temple where we preserve the ancient rites of the Sun God shall be put to death!

Be put to death! ... D'you really think we'll let ourselves be massacred, just like that, you tin-hatted tyrant?!

Captain, please! Keep quiet!

Noble Prince of the Sun, I crave your indulgence. Let me tell you our story. We have never sought to commit sacrilege. We were simply looking for our friend, Professor Calculus ...

Your friend dared to wear the sacred bracelet of Rascar Capac. Your friend will likewise be put to death!

Blistering barnacles, you've no right to kill him! No more than you have a right to kill us, thundering typhoons! It's murder, pure and simple!

But it is not we who will put you to death. It is the Sun himself, for his rays will set alight the pyre for which you are destined.

As for this young Indian who guided these strangers and thus betrayed his race, he will suffer the penalty reserved for traitors! ... He will be sacrificed immediately on the altar of the Sun God!

Billions of blue blistering barnacles! The first one who touches a hair of that boy's head is a dead duck!

Grrr! ...

Great snakes! I just remembered! Your medal, Zorrino! ... Show them!

?

Where did you steal that, little viper?

I not steal, noble Prince of the Sun, I not steal! ... He give me this medal! ... I not steal!

And you, foreign dog, where did you get it? Like others of your kind, you robbed the tombs of our ancestors no doubt!

Noble Prince of the Sun, I beg leave to speak ...

!

49

It is I, noble Prince of the Sun, who gave the sacred token to this young stranger.

You, Huascar? . . . A high priest of the Sun God, you committed sacrilege and gave this talisman to an enemy of our race?

He is not an enemy of our race, nobel Prince of the Sun . . . with my own eyes I saw him go alone to the defence of this boy, when the child was being ill-treated by two of those vile foreigners whom we hate. For that reason, knowing that he would face other great dangers, I gave him the token. Did I do wrong, illustrious Prince?

No, Huascar, you did nobly. But your action will save only this young Indian, for his life is protected by the talisman.

It will not save the young stranger: by his generosity he forfeited his only safeguard. Our laws are explicit: he will be put to death with his companion.

Nevertheless, I will grant them one favour . . .

I knew it: his bark's worse than his bite!

It is this: Within the next thirty days, they must die. But they may choose the day and the hour when the rays of the sacred Sun will light their pyre.

. . . They must give their answer tomorrow. As for this young Indian, he will be separated from his companions and his life will be spared. But he will stay within our temple until he dies, lest our secrets be divulged.

Now, let the strangers be taken away and kept in close confinement until tomorrow. The Prince of the Sun has spoken!

Well, we're in up to our necks, this time!

I know . . . But I'm glad Zorrino's safe, anyway.

Bunch of savages! . . . What I need is a pipe to calm my nerves . . . Where is it? . . . Ah, got it . . . Hello, what's this?

Oh yes, I remember . . . the newspaper we saved to light a fire.

Well, we shan't be needing that now . . . There'll be a fire all right . . .

But, thundering typhoons, we shan't be lighting it!

How do we get out of here?

These bars, perhaps? . . .
No, they're firmly fixed . . .

Anyway, even if we did manage to shift them, this window overlooks a precipice.

Blistering barnacles! I've lost my matches!

Give me your pipe, Captain. I've got a little magnifying-glass.

A magnifying-glass?

Why, it's alight!

Yes, look . . . that's done it.

Easy as winking! . . . It's amazing! . . . Marvellous!

Marvellous, yes . . . And that's precisely how the Incas will light up their bonfire when they set about roasting us.

. . . Unless they use parabolic mirrors, like Archimedes when he burnt the Roman ships beseiging Syracuse.

My pipe!

My pipe! . . . My poor pipe! . . . Blistering barnacles, it's broken!

Hello, Snowy, what are you doing? Where did you find that paper?

Meanwhile, in Europe . . .

We've searched South America from top to bottom, sir, without result. We lost all trace of Tintin, the Captain and the Professor.

To be precise: we got lost.

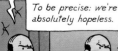

We have now decided to undertake a fresh search using entirely new methods. It's the only way: otherwise we have absolutely no hope.

To be precise: we're absolutely hopeless.

I see . . . And what are you new methods?

You must allow us to preserve absolute secrecy, sir . . . "Dumb's the word": that's our motto.

Dowsing, my dear Thompson, like Professor Calculus; that'll put us on their track.

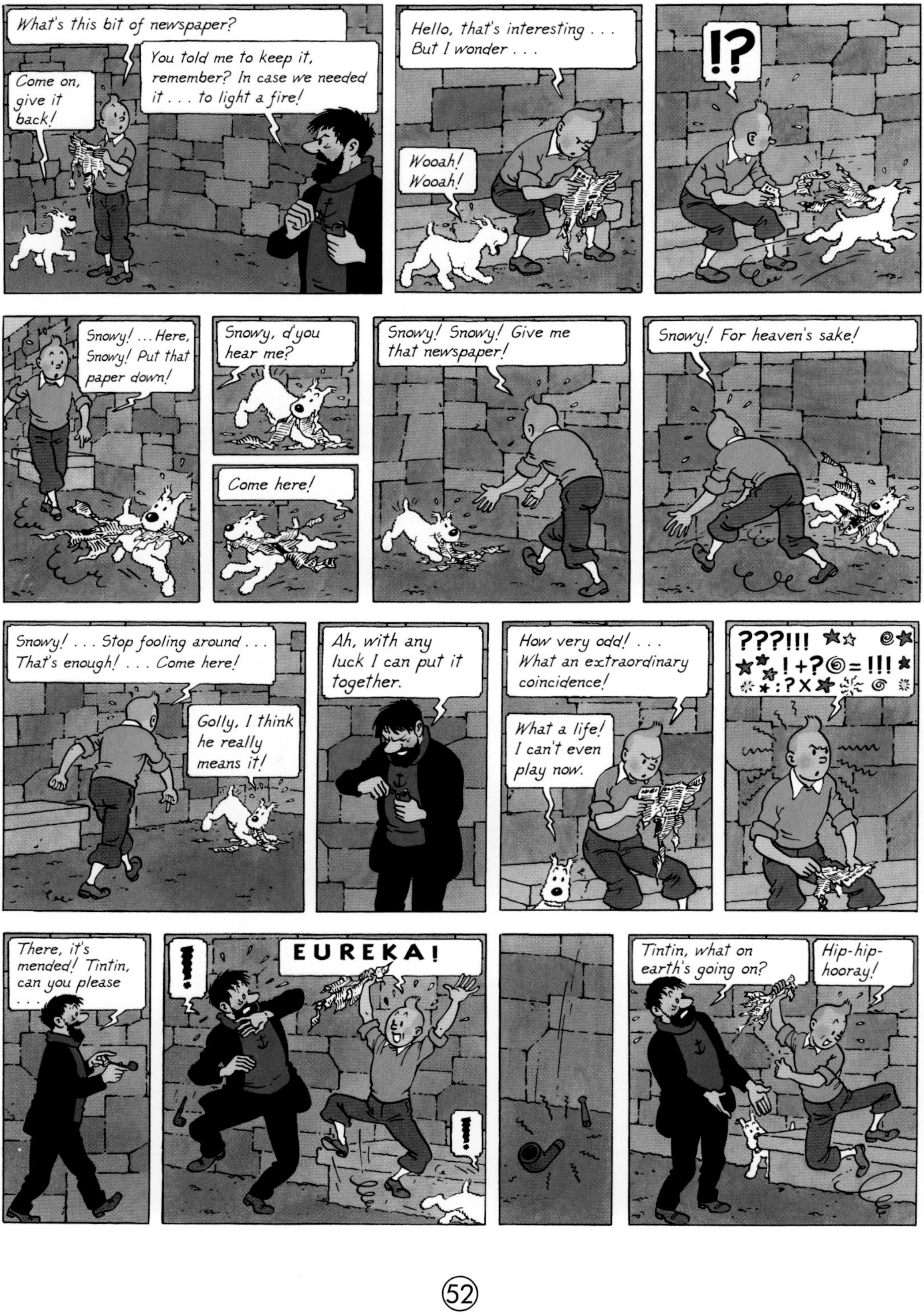

What's this bit of newspaper?
Come on, give it back!
You told me to keep it, remember? In case we needed it . . . to light a fire!
Hello, that's interesting . . . But I wonder . . .
Wooah! Wooah!
!?
Snowy! ... Here, Snowy! Put that paper down!
Snowy, d'you hear me?
Come here!
Snowy! Snowy! Give me that newspaper!
Snowy! For heaven's sake!
Snowy! . . . Stop fooling around . . . That's enough! . . . Come here!
Golly, I think he really means it!
Ah, with any luck I can put it together.
How very odd! . . . What an extraordinary coincidence!
What a life! I can't even play now.
???!!! ! +? = !!! : ? X
There, it's mended! Tintin, can you please . . .
!
EUREKA!
!
Tintin, what on earth's going on?
Hip-hip-hooray!

Captain! Captain! We're saved!

Saved? . . . What do you mean?

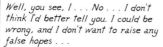

Well, you see, I . . . No . . . I don't think I'd better tell you. I could be wrong, and I don't want to raise any false hopes . . .

But I . . .

Listen, Captain: you must trust me, and promise to do exactly as I say, without hesitation. You'll understand later on.

Well, yes, but . . .

Yes? . . . Good: that's a promise! . . . Now we must be patient . . . While we're waiting I'll mend your pipe . . .

Meanwhile . . .

Why, they aren't here! . . . How peculiar! The pendulum definitely indicates that they are somewhere high up.

The next morning . . .

Well, strangers; have you decided upon the day and the hour of your death?

Yes, noble Prince of the Sun . . . I wish . . . we wish to die in . . . er . . . eighteen days' time, at 11 o'clock . . . It is my friend's birthday, and . . .

Tintin, you're crazy! . . . You know it isn't . . .

Quiet, Captain! . . . You promised to trust me.

So be it! . . . In eighteen days, at the hour you have chosen, you shall atone for your crime. Guards, take them away. Let them be well treated, and let their least wish be granted!

A few minutes later . . .

Here, señores. You stay in royal apartment now . . .

Now, will you kindly explain what this is all about?

Not yet, Captain, not yet. But you can be sure of one thing: there's nothing to worry about!

Nothing to worry about! . . . Not a sausage! . . . We're only going to be roasted alive in eighteen days' time: apart from that there's nothing to worry about! . . . To be precise, as Thompson and Thomson would say, nothing at all!

Time goes by . . .

Only seven more days . . . Thundering typhoons, we're in a real jam!

Next morning . . .

How can we get out? . . . Who can help us? . . . Zorrino, perhaps . . .

The next day . . .

It's a fine time for gymnastics! Blistering barnacles, here we are with five days to live, and you do morning exercises!

Why not, Captain? One must keep fit.

Keep fit! Keep fit! . . . Thundering typhoons! I don't need exercises to keep me fit! . . . I'll show you just how fit I am: at my age, too!

Watch this: a standing jump, feet together, clean over the table.

HUP!

My, my!

!

So you think that's funny, eh?

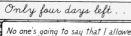
Only four days left . . .

No one's going to say that I allowed myself to be roasted like a turkey on a spit! . . . We must do something!

You know quite well that's impossible.

Only three days . . .

What can we do, thundering typhoons!?

Round and round . . . he's making me giddy!

Only two days to go . . .

How can you lie there, just lounging around! . . . Billions of blistering barnacles! We must do something!

Trust me, Captain. In two days' time we'll be free.

One day left . . .

It's all over! . . . Nothing to hope for! I never knew things could look so black!

At that moment . . .

According to the pendulum they're very low . . .

Next morning . . .

Only a few hours to live, and all you can do is read that bit of newspaper for the hundredth time!

". . . The Swiss expedition is on its way to the Western Cordillera in the Andes. It will . . ." The rest is torn away.

Blistering barnacles! If it weren't for these confounded bars I'd soon be out of here!

CRACK
BANG
BOOM
?

We're free! . . . Tintin, we're free! . . . Come on quickly, hurry! . . . Out!

Don't do it, Captain! You'll break your neck!

Aha! We are just in time!

Thundering typhoons! . . . Too late!

The hour has come! You will put on the sacrificial robe.

Me? Put on that Patagonian petticoat? Never!

It is our law. You must obey!

Never! d'you hear? . . . And when I say never, I mean never!

Captain, please . . .

Let him be robed for the sacrifice.

CRASH

Never!

CRACK

BOOM

You think I'm going to be the guy on your bonfire? . . . Never!

Whatever happens, I'm getting out of this madhouse!

!

Nothing broken, I hope, Captain?

Unless I'm much mistaken, there's something very fishy going on.

BOOM ? BOOM BOOM

I wonder what that music is?

If you call it that!

BOOM BOOM BOOM BOOM

Pacharurac – Pachacamac
Viracocha

Cayhinapac Churasunqui Camasunqui

Captain, there's Professor Calculus! . . . Old Cuthbert, after our long search! . . . Here he comes. They're going to tie him up beside us.

Why, Captain! . . . What a delightful surprise! . . . How are you?

Very well, thanks, as you can see!

And you too, my dear Tintin! . . . I'm so pleased to see you again! . . . But tell me, what is all this performance? . . . Where are we?

With the Incas . . .

Ah, the cinema! . . . Good, I quite understand . . . Some historical drama, no doubt . . . Those people there are dressed like . . . like Aztecs, I think . . . Or rather, I should say, Incas.

Incas, exactly. Now you've got it.

Yes, their make-up is perfect . . . And look at those dancers: so natural: who'd believe they are acting.

Supposing I'm wrong . . .

Noble Prince, it is the hour of sacrifice!

Meanwhile . . .

According to the pendulum, they should be in a very hot spot . . .

Let the sacrifice begin!
. . . Let the High Priest
of the Sun advance to
the pyre!

What's that thing he's got there?

That's the burning glass
to set our bonfire alight.

No?

Let me go! You mustn't
kill them!

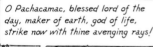

O Pachacamac, blessed lord of the
day, maker of earth, god of life,
strike now with thine avenging rays!

Stay, Huascar! . . .
The Sun God will not
hear your prayers!

?   ?   Grrr!

O magnificent
Sun, if it is
thy will that
we should
live, give us
now a sign!

Silence, foreign dog!
How dare you call
upon the Sun?

O God of the Sun, sublime
Pachacamac, display thy
power. I implore thee! . . .
If this sacrifice is not thy
will, hide thy shining face
from us!

Poor Tintin, he's gone
off his head!

Not at all: your hat
is very chic.

I thank thee,
supreme majesty!
My prayer is
answered; the
darkness moves
across thy face.

But . . . blistering
barnacles, he's
right! . . . Have I
gone crazy too?
. . . It's magic!

!

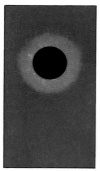

Next day . . .

I keep my word, noble strangers: you are free . . . My men will escort you to the foot of the mountains.

Thank you, noble Prince, but I have one further request . . .

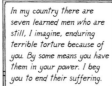
In my country there are seven learned men who are still, I imagine, enduring terrible torture because of you. By some means you have them in your power. I beg you to end their suffering.

These men came here like hyenas, violating our tombs and plundering our sacred treasures. They deserve the punishment I have meted out.

No, they did not come to plunder, noble Prince of the Sun. Their sole purpose was to make known to the world your ancient customs and the splendours of your civilisation.

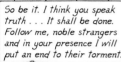
So be it. I think you speak truth . . . It shall be done. Follow me, noble strangers and in your presence I will put an end to their torment.

Each of these images represents one of the men for whom you plead. Here in this chamber, by our hidden powers, we have tortured them. It is here that we will release them from their punishment.

Witchcraft! . . . I can't believe it! . . . But the crystal balls: what were they for?

The crystal balls contained a mystic liquid, obtained from coca, which plunged the victims into a deep sleep. The High Priest cast his spell over them . . . and could use them as he willed.

Now I see it all! . . . That explains the seven crystal balls, and the extraordinary illness of the explorers. Each time the High Priest tortured the wax images the explorers suffered those terrible agonies.

Destroy the images, Huaco!

At that moment, in Europe . . .

What am I doing here?

What's happened? . . . How did I get into hospital? . . .

Where are we, Carling?

That's what I'm wondering, Sanders.

You here, Reedbuck?

Clarkson! . . . What in the world . . .

How did I get here?

60

Next morning . . .

So you've chosen to stay here, Zorrino . . . We must say goodbye, then. Perhaps one day we shall meet again . . .

Adios, amigo Tintin!

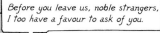

Before you leave us, noble strangers, I too have a favour to ask of you.

I know, noble Prince of the Sun, and you need have no fears about that . . .

I swear that I will never reveal to anyone the whereabouts of the Temple of the Sun!

Me too, old salt, I swear too! . . . May my rum be rationed and my beard be barbecued if I breathe so much as a word!

Me too; I swear I will never act in another film, however glittering the contract Hollywood may offer me. You have my word.

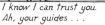

I know I can trust you. Ah, your guides . . .

Blistering barnacles! More llamas!

Perhaps you would like to open one of the saddlebags?

! !

Thundering typhoons! . . . It's fantastic! . . . Gold! . . . Diamonds! . . . Precious stones! . . .

!

We thank you, noble Prince of the Sun, but we cannot accept such magnificent gifts.

Unless you absolutely insist . . .

Oh, they are nothing compared to the riches of the temple! . . . Since I have your promise of silence, come with me . . .

? !

Enter!

Meanwhile . . .

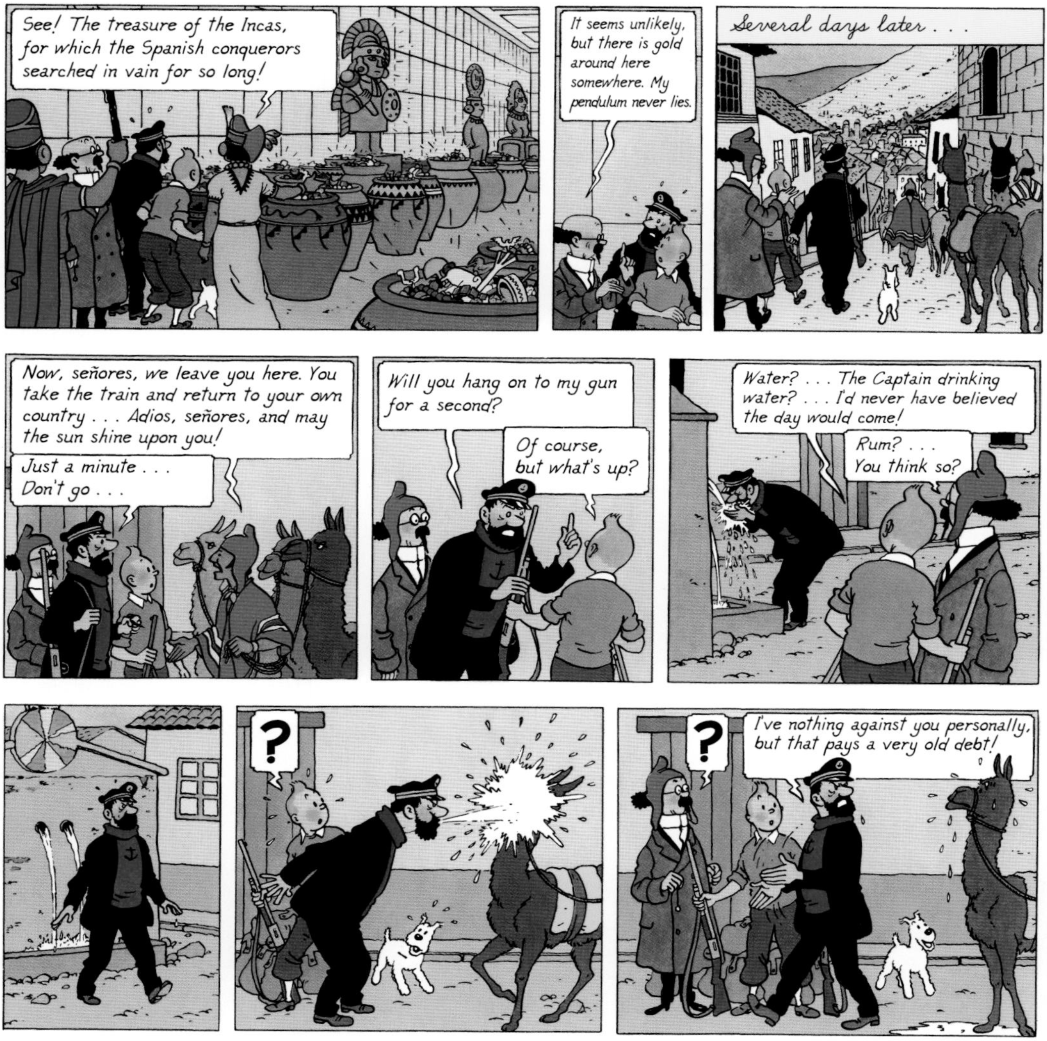
See! The treasure of the Incas, for which the Spanish conquerors searched in vain for so long!
It seems unlikely, but there is gold around here somewhere. My pendulum never lies.
Several days later . . .
Now, señores, we leave you here. You take the train and return to your own country . . . Adios, señores, and may the sun shine upon you!
Just a minute . . . Don't go . . .
Will you hang on to my gun for a second?
Of course, but what's up?
Water? . . . The Captain drinking water? . . . I'd never have believed the day would come!
Rum? . . . You think so?
?
?
I've nothing against you personally, but that pays a very old debt!

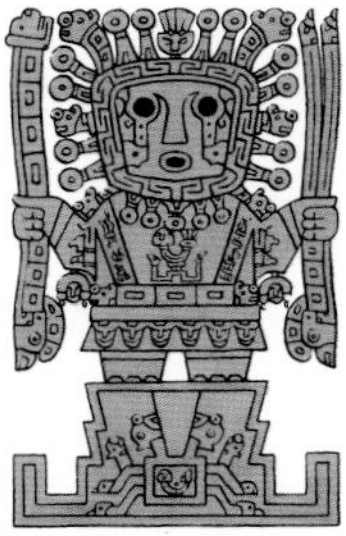

THE END

THE REAL-LIFE INSPIRATION BEHIND TINTIN'S ADVENTURES

Written by Stuart Tett
with the collaboration of Studio Moulinsart.

Discover something new and exciting

HERGÉ

Reading

Hergé liked to read. In an interview in 1978, he said, "When I was a teenager I read my first real book, *The Three Musketeers*. Dumas is a wonderful storyteller, who knows how to find the perfect mix between adventure and feelings."

Hergé mainly read from two sources of information while researching ancient Incan culture for *Prisoners of the Sun*: the book *Perou et Bolivie* (1880) by Charles Wiener and a long, richly illustrated article entitled "The Incas: Empire Builders of the Andes" in an issue of *National Geographic* magazine dated February 1938.

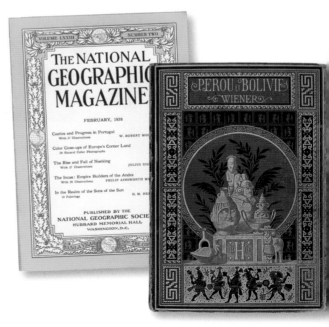

about Tintin and his creator Hergé!

TINTIN

Bravery

In *Prisoners of the Sun*, Tintin saves Zorrino from a cowardly attack by two men. The brave reporter always stands up for the victims of aggression—on the left you can see the moment in *The Blue Lotus* when Tintin snaps the cane of another bully.

After writing Tintin's adventure in China, Hergé drew a picture in the December 23, 1937 issue of *Le Petit Vingtième*, to keep readers informed about the suffering of the Chinese during the second Sino-Japanese war (1937-1945).

THE TRUE STORY
…behind *Prisoners of the Sun*

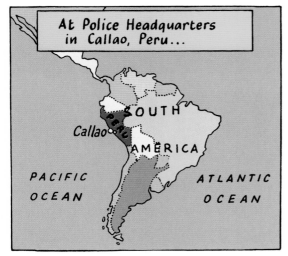

Right at the start of *Prisoners of the Sun*, a map of South America shows us the country of Peru, where Tintin and Captain Haddock will search for Professor Calculus. Peru is home to the Andes mountain range, which we will explore later.

Once upon a time…

The first page of the story was published in the December 19, 1946 issue of the new *Tintin* magazine (see the Young Readers *The Seven Crystal Balls* to read more about the magazine). The cover of this issue shows Tintin growing bigger — because the magazine was increasing to sixteen pages long!

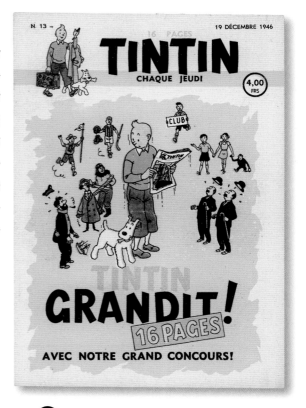

A letter to Tintin

Readers of *Tintin* magazine could send letters to Tintin himself! To post a letter to their favorite hero, they didn't even have to write an address: Tintin was so popular that all they had to do was to write, "Tintin, Brussels," on the envelope and the postman would know where to deliver it.

Above and below you can see the drawings Hergé made for the mail column in the magazine. You can also see some of the replies (which have been translated into English) that Tintin wrote to letters about the new Tintin club, and questions he received from readers.

R. & L. BLACKBURN, Todmorgen (Lancashire), Britain— We are really happy to count you among the first English members of our club. A welcome handshake for you!

ANDRE GOFFERD, Aywaille— Thank you for your jokes. Unfortunately we don't have a place to publish them in the magazine!

R. FREGNIEUX, Charleroi— Your idea is quite good and we have passed it on to Professor Calculus who will write about it in one of his next columns.

NICOLLE VERVEUX— We will try to put more games in the magazine as you ask. Please be patient!

Watching ships

Captain Haddock uses some binoculars to get a close-up view of the ship the *Pachacamac*. "Thundering typhoons!" She's flying flags to indicate infectious disease on board. *The Pachacamac* will be quarantined and forced to stay out of the harbor.

Once upon a time...

Speaking of ships, Hergé loved to educate his readers, and *Tintin* magazine gave him and his team the opportunity to teach all kinds of interesting and exciting things. He drew a series of pictures for the magazine showing historical ships such as the Roman galley shown below. The caption is a translation of the text that accompanied the drawing.

The Romans followed the Greeks and the Carthaginians when it came to naval warfare. But they did invent a new weapon, named the *corvus*, a boarding device with an iron spike that pierced the enemy deck, immobilizing the ship. The first permanent flotilla was created under Emperor Augustus. Roman admirals were called *praefecti*; lower commanding officers had titles such as *centurion*, *trierarchus* and *nauarchus*.

The page of the story with the moment when Haddock watches the *Pachacamac* through his binoculars was published in the first 1947 issue of *Tintin* magazine (January 2). The front cover of this issue is shown below. To celebrate the New Year, Hergé drew a mix of real people and comic strip characters attending a wonderful feast. Can you spot Hergé and his assistant Edgar Pierre Jacobs sitting on the right hand side?

Brother and sister
Jo and Zette
are the star characters
of another series
created by Hergé.
They go on
their adventures
along with their pet
monkey, Jocko
(next to Tintin).

Corentin
is a comic strip
character whose
stories were published
in *Tintin* magazine.
His creator, Paul Cuvelier,
is sitting just to the right.

Jacques Laudy
was another author who
created comic strips
that were published
in *Tintin* magazine.
Laudy loved to play
the bagpipes; you can see
a set on the back
of his chair!

Tintin in disguise

After Tintin discovered that Professor Calculus was on board the *Pachacamac*, the kidnappers took the professor to shore and set off, with Tintin following close behind. Captain Haddock has been trying to catch up and stops to ask a local if he has met Tintin on the way.

Preparatory pencil sketch by Hergé.

Once upon a time…

Two pages ago you saw the picture of a Roman ship with Tintin dressed up as a Roman soldier that Hergé drew for his readers. Together with his assistant, Edgar Pierre Jacobs, Hergé planned to create a series of drawings to help children learn about all kinds of vehicles and also about historical dress. In the end, the series on historical dress was never published, but you can see some of the drawings Hergé did below and on the next page!

As Tintin and Haddock continue their search for Professor Calculus, they go deeper and deeper into the country of Peru.

The drawing below shows Tintin wearing the helmet and armor typically used by a Spanish soldier of the sixteenth century. The Spanish invaded Peru during this century and took control of the Inca Empire, leading to the demise of the Incas.

Remember, Hergé only drew these pictures to teach about how clothing looked hundreds of years ago. In this story, Tintin has quite the opposite attitude from the Spanish *conquistadors* (conquerors) of the sixteenth century—he wants to help the Incas preserve their civilization!

Now let's **Explore and Discover!**

EXPLORE AND DISCOVER

Tintin, Snowy and Captain Haddock took the train to Jauga, following the kidnappers of Professor Calculus. But their carriage was sabotaged and ran away! Captain Haddock jumped out already, but now the carriage is going too fast for Tintin and Snowy to follow. There's only one thing for it: a leap into the river at the bottom of a ravine!

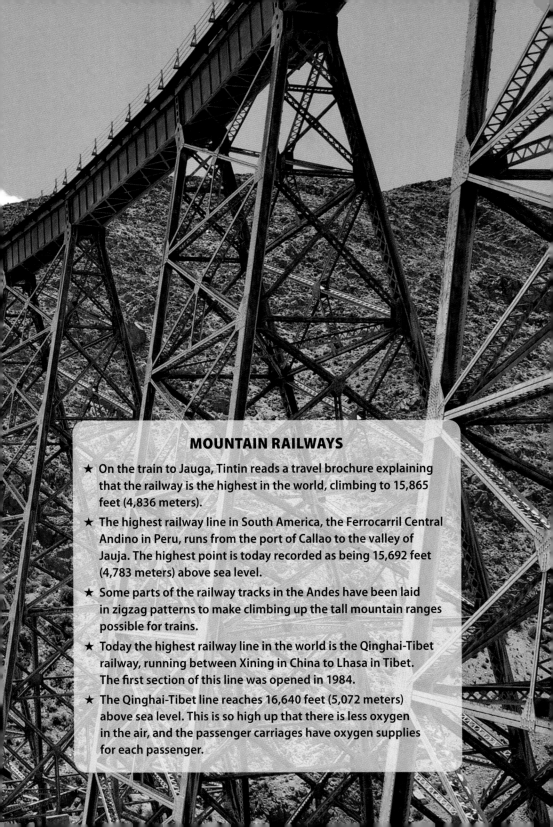

MOUNTAIN RAILWAYS

★ On the train to Jauga, Tintin reads a travel brochure explaining that the railway is the highest in the world, climbing to 15,865 feet (4,836 meters).

★ The highest railway line in South America, the Ferrocarril Central Andino in Peru, runs from the port of Callao to the valley of Jauja. The highest point is today recorded as being 15,692 feet (4,783 meters) above sea level.

★ Some parts of the railway tracks in the Andes have been laid in zigzag patterns to make climbing up the tall mountain ranges possible for trains.

★ Today the highest railway line in the world is the Qinghai-Tibet railway, running between Xining in China to Lhasa in Tibet. The first section of this line was opened in 1984.

★ The Qinghai-Tibet line reaches 16,640 feet (5,072 meters) above sea level. This is so high up that there is less oxygen in the air, and the passenger carriages have oxygen supplies for each passenger.

ZORRINO

When Tintin and Captain Haddock arrive in the small town of Jauga, no matter who they turn to, they can't make any headway in their search for Professor Calculus. Then, when Tintin protects a young Peruvian orange seller from bullies, the boy is so touched that he decides to help the brave reporter find his friend.

Zorrino becomes devoted to Tintin and Captain Haddock, and later on in the story Tintin gives up his only safeguard against an Inca death sentence so that Zorrino is spared.

The friendship between Zorrino and Tintin is reminiscent of the friendship between Tintin and Chang Chong-chen, the Chinese boy Tintin meets in *The Blue Lotus*, based on the real Chinese student who helped in the creation of this story, whom Hergé met in 1934. You can read about Chang in the Young Readers Edition of that story.

LLAMAS

To help them in their long journey through the Andes, Zorrino has brought along two llamas to carry supplies. Captain Haddock still remembers his rather unfortunate run-in with one of the animals at the beginning of the story!

★ Llamas are domesticated South American animals related to camels. They have been used by people in the Andes for meat and to carry goods since the time of the Inca Empire (1400-1532 AD).

★ Llamas are herbivores, eating ferns and grass. Typically a llama's lifespan is between twenty and thirty years.

★ Although they are used to carry goods and supplies, llamas are stubborn animals. If the load is too heavy, a llama will refuse to move until some is taken off.

★ Llamas can be used to look after herds of sheep. They can bond well when introduced to the animals, and will then survey the sheep, alerting and protecting them from predators.

CONDOR ATTACK!

I've got a real bird's eye view!

As Tintin, Captain Haddock and Zorrino trek higher into the Andes Mountains, they have a run-in with a sinister group of men. But just as Tintin has gotten the better of the gang, a new danger appears from the skies. A condor swoops down and snatches Snowy!

★ The Andean condor is one of the largest flying birds in the world. It can weigh up to over thirty pounds and have a wingspan up to 10 feet (3 meters).

★ With such large wings, condors can soar on air currents for long periods of time without expending too much energy flapping.

★ The condor in the story decides that Snowy will make a tasty meal and in real life condors will eat animals of Snowy's size, although they prefer to feed on the carcasses of larger animals, such as cows or deer.

★ Hergé drew Snowy tucking into some bones in the condor's nest, but in reality, Andean condors do not make nests. They perch high up on the mountainside and lay eggs in small caves or crevices.

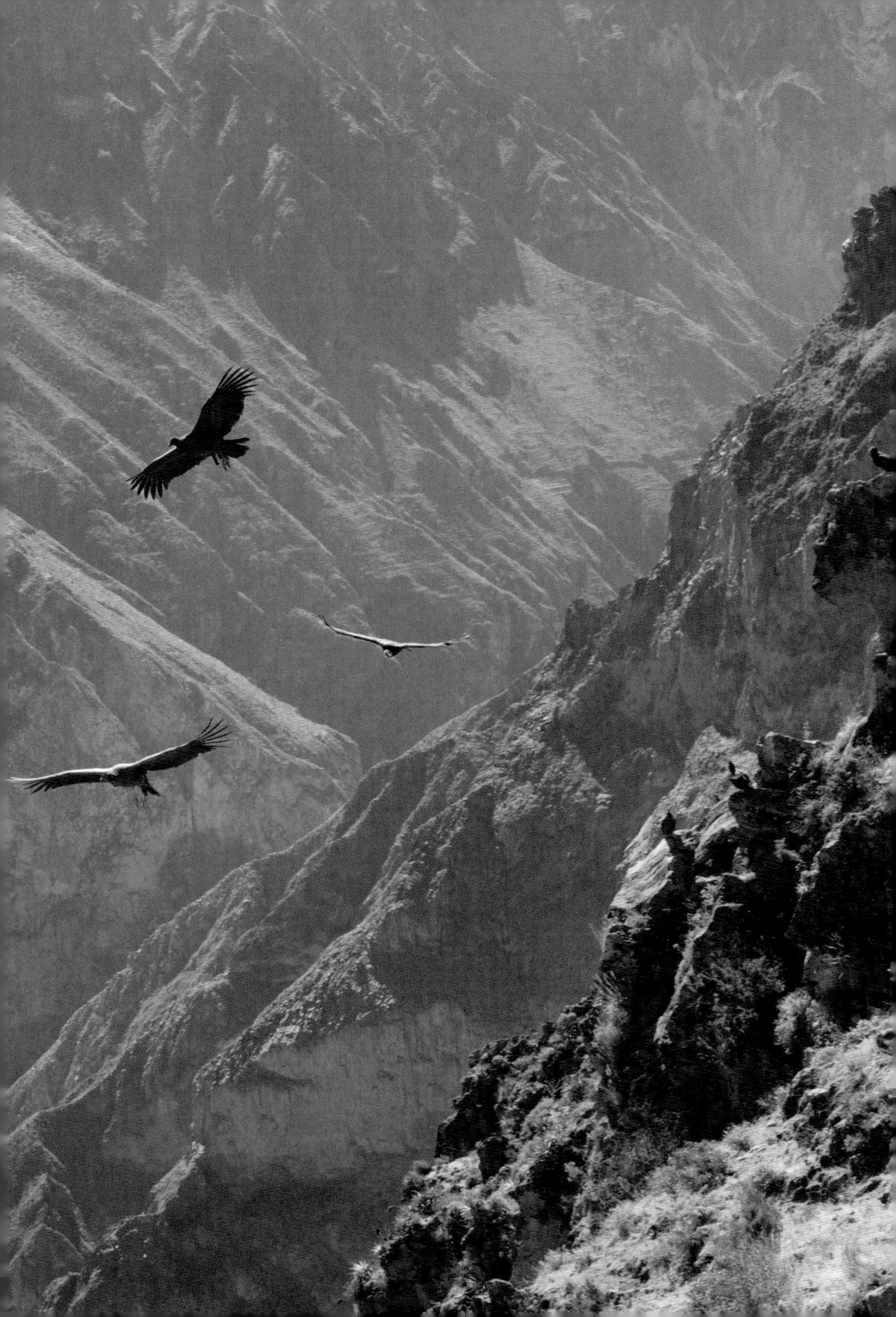

THE JUNGLE

After further dangerous events including a lucky escape from an avalanche, Tintin, Captain Haddock and Zorrino start to make their way through thick jungle. While there wasn't much wildlife on the snowy mountain peaks, the hot, humid jungle lower down is teeming with life!

Anteaters are solitary animals.
They do not have teeth, but with their long,
sticky tongues they can eat tens
of thousands of ants a day!

The closest animal relatives to tapirs are rhinoceroses and horses. Tapirs are herbivores, eating fruit and leaves. A group of tapirs together is called a "candle."

Pythons are one of the largest snakes in the world, growing up to over thirty feet (10 meters) in length. They are not poisonous; instead they kill their prey by squeezing it to death.

Alligators are reptiles that can weigh as much as a car (up to 1,000 pounds). They can grow up to around 15 feet (4.5 meters) long. They have shorter, more U-shaped heads than crocodiles.

ANCIENT TOMB

After their trek through the jungle, Tintin discovers a hidden entrance to the Inca Temple of the Sun. As they go deeper into the tunnel, Tintin comes across an ancient tomb.

Remember that Hergé read *Perou et Bolivie* (1880) by Charles Wiener to research his story? Look at one of the illustrations from this book. The caption in the book reads, "Cloth mummy head filled with seaweed, found at Chancay."

Tintin thinks that the caves that they have discovered are so old that the Incas have forgotten them. The vase he knocks over by accident is certainly older than Inca culture. It dates to between 200-500 AD, the Early Intermediate period of the South American pre-Inca Moche culture.

MAKING FIRE

Why, it's alight!

Yes, look... that's done it.

Tintin helps Captain Haddock to light his pipe with the aid of a magnifying glass...and then makes a sobering remark that makes the captain drop his pipe. Tintin carries on, ruminating about other possible methods by which the Incas might go about carrying out their execution.

Marvellous, yes... And that's precisely how the Incas will light up their bonfire when they set about roasting us.

....Unless they use parabolic mirrors, like Archimedes when he burnt the Roman ships beseiging Syracuse.

My pipe!

Hergé drew this picture of Tintin looking like Archimedes to go alongside one of the ships he drew to educate children (see page 6). Note the Archimedes screw! Hergé loved to draw accurate details, but today we are not certain that Archimedes had a quiff on top of his head.

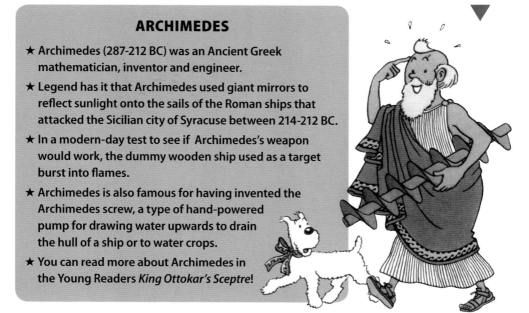

ARCHIMEDES

★ Archimedes (287-212 BC) was an Ancient Greek mathematician, inventor and engineer.

★ Legend has it that Archimedes used giant mirrors to reflect sunlight onto the sails of the Roman ships that attacked the Sicilian city of Syracuse between 214-212 BC.

★ In a modern-day test to see if Archimedes's weapon would work, the dummy wooden ship used as a target burst into flames.

★ Archimedes is also famous for having invented the Archimedes screw, a type of hand-powered pump for drawing water upwards to drain the hull of a ship or to water crops.

★ You can read more about Archimedes in the Young Readers *King Ottokar's Sceptre*!

THE INCAS

Tintin and Captain Haddock are led out to the pyre on which they will be sacrificed. It would be enthralling to be surrounded by all the authentic Inca décor if you weren't about to be burned as an offering to the sun!

Hergé copied elements from a black-and-white photo of the fifteenth-century Inca site of Machu Picchu, published in *National Geographic* magazine. His drawing was colored to represent as faithfully as possible the real clothing that was worn by the Incas hundreds of years ago, and the portrayal of the buildings at Machu Picchu is so accurate that there is no need to show a photo of the real location!

MACHU PICCHU

★ The site of Machu Picchu is located high up in the Andes Mountains in Peru, 2,430 meters above sea level.

★ The site first became known to the western world when it was discovered in 1911 by American explorer Hiram Bingham III. He was actually looking for another lost Inca city known as Vilcabamba at the time.

★ Archaeologists say that Machu Picchu was built as an estate for Inca royalty.

★ The Incas built the walls and buildings using their own special method, *ashlar*, where blocks of stone were cut into shapes that fit together so precisely that no mortar or cement was needed to bind them together.

★ The ashlar technique resulted in buildings that are highly resistant to earthquakes, regular events in Peru. During an earthquake the stones in a building are said to "dance": they bounce among themselves as the ground shakes and then fall back into place.

★ If you go back a few pages to page 13, you can see part of Machu Picchu behind the llamas!

ECLIPSE

Par son mouvement dans le ciel, la lune
promène son cône d'ombre sur l'Europe.

In English, the French caption reads:
"As it moves through the sky, the moon's
shadow moves across Europe."

In the April 8, 1948 issue of *Tintin* magazine—including the comic strips showing the eclipse that saves the lives of Tintin, Captain Haddock and Professor Calculus —a page explaining this real-life phenomenon was published. As well as a more lengthy explanation, a sentence resumed the key point: "An eclipse happens every time that the moon passes in front of the sun."

INCA GOLD

Earlier you read about the Spanish invasion of the Inca Empire hundreds of years ago. Besides their desire to create a colony in South America, the Spanish also ransacked the population for their gold and silver, of which plentiful reserves had been mined from the Andes Mountains by the Incas.

After releasing the members of the Sanders-Hardiman expedition from the curse that has plagued them since the story of *The Seven Crystal Balls*, the Prince of the Sun shows Tintin and his friends some of the treasures the Spanish didn't find.

TINTIN'S GRAND ADVENTURE

The publication of the book *Prisoners of the Sun* marked the end of Hergé's latest two-part story; it would not be long before he would undertake another two-part adventure, which would see Tintin and his friends travel to the Moon! But first he had some unfinished business to attend to: a story that he had abandoned when World War II started, *Land of Black Gold*.

Trivia: *Prisoners of the Sun*

When Tintin jumps out of the train in the Andes, he is lucky to land in the water. In real life it looks like he might be jumping out too late, because, as the train is moving so fast, he would not simply fall downward but would also keep moving sideways, and would crash into other side of the valley!

Hergé regretted showing the Incas fooled by the eclipse, as in reality the Incas were quite advanced astronomers and they probably knew about eclipses.

Hergé used the name of a real Inca temple, the Pachacamac, for the ship in the story as well as for the sun god called upon by Tintin and the Incas.

The *Tintin* magazine columns showing Tintin in different historical dress next to ships looked so good that the series developed into an independent project covering aircraft, automobiles and hot-air balloons. Eventually several books of these drawings with short accompanying articles were published between 1978 and 1981 under the collective title Voir et Savoir (See and Know).

The original cover for *Prisoners of the Sun* (1949)

GO ON MORE ADVENTURES WITH TINTIN!

THE SECRET OF THE UNICORN

RED RACKHAM'S TREASURE

CIGARS OF THE PHARAOH

THE BLUE LOTUS

TINTIN IN AMERICA

THE BROKEN EAR

THE BLACK ISLAND

KING OTTOKAR'S SCEPTRE

THE CRAB WITH THE GOLDEN CLAWS

THE SHOOTING STAR

THE SEVEN CRYSTAL BALLS

PRISONERS OF THE SUN

ALSO AVAILABLE